ni hao, kai-lan

Kai-lan's Great Trip to China

adapted by Mickie Matheis

based on the screenplay written by Sascha Paladino and Bradley Zweig

illustrated by Toby Williams

Simon Spotlight/Nickelodeon
New York   London   Toronto   Sydney

Ni hao! I'm Kai-lan.
Look—the sun fuzzies are making a path!
Let's see where they're going. *Gen wo lai*—
follow me!

The sun fuzzies are leading to my grandpa's house! I call him YeYe.

YeYe's talking to my favorite great-aunt on a videophone! I call her Gu nai nai. She is YeYe's sister.

"Kai-lan, *ni hao!*" says Gu nai nai. "Would you and your friends like to visit me in China? When you get here, you can meet a baby panda."

We'd *love* to visit you in China, Gu nai nai! See you soon! *Zai jian*—good-bye!

I feel so happy about going to China! *Kai xin!* That means "happy." Say "*kai xin!*"

I'm bringing my heart box with me. I put things in here that make my heart feel super happy. *Kai xin!*

We made it to China! And here's Gu nai nai! Gu nai nai, *ni hao!* These are my friends.

"*Wo jiao* Tolee!" says Tolee. That means, "My name is Tolee."

"*Wo jiao* Rintoo!" says Rintoo. That means, "My name is Rintoo."

"*Wo jiao* Hoho!" says Hoho. That means, "My name is Hoho."

"It's very nice to meet all of you," says Gu nai nai. "Let's go to my home. Later we'll go see the baby panda."

On our way to Gu nai nai's house we stop by a noodle stand for a snack. The noodles smell yummy! *Hao xiang!* Uh-oh. Rintoo and Hoho aren't eating their noodles. They are scared to try a new type of food. What should you do when you're scared to try something new?

When you're scared of something new,
here is what you can do.
Just try it, try it, try it.
Because you might like it!

Rintoo and Hoho try some of their noodles—and they like them!
Xie xie, Gu nai nai! Thank you for the delicious noodles.

When we get to Gu nai nai's house, she gives us
special slippers to wear. Rintoo and Hoho love their slippers!
Uh-oh. Tolee isn't wearing his slippers. He likes his panda
slippers and is scared to try on new ones. What should you
do when you're scared to try something new?

When you're scared of something new,
here is what you can do.
Just try it, try it, try it.
Because you might like it!

Tolee tries on the slippers—and he likes them!
Xie xie, Gu nai nai! Thank you for the slippers.

Gu nai nai says it's time to meet the baby panda. That makes us happy. *Kai xin!*

Do you see the baby panda? There he is—in that tree house with his mommy. He's eating watermelon! *Ni hao*, baby panda! *Wo jiao* Kai-lan. My name is Kai-lan.

"Wo jiao Tolee!" says Tolee.
"Wo jiao Rintoo!" says Rintoo.
"Wo jiao Hoho!" says Hoho.
The baby panda is getting his name tonight at a special party. I have an idea! Let's bring presents to the panda's party. Will you help us find presents for the baby panda? Super! Let's go, go, go!

Hoho wants to get the baby panda a watermelon blanket because the baby panda loves to eat watermelon. This blanket is going to make the baby panda's heart feel super happy. *Kai xin!*

Let's put the blanket in my heart box.

Rintoo wants to get little tiger shoes for the baby panda. Gu nai nai says we can get them at a store on a nearby island. We need to take a boat to get there.

Uh-oh. The baby panda won't go on board. He's scared to get on the boat.

We gotta, gotta try
to find the reason why
the baby panda is scared to get on the boat!

Do you think the baby panda won't get on the boat because he's scared of trying something new? I think so too.

What can we try?
It's up to me and you.
The baby panda won't ride in the boat!
We'll figure out what to do!

Hoho, Rintoo, and Tolee were scared to try new things. But when they tried them, they liked them!

When you're scared of something new, here is what you can do. Just try it, try it, try it. Because you might like it!

Look—the baby panda tried something new. He got on the boat! He likes riding in the boat. It makes him happy! *Kai xin!*

Rintoo picks out a pair of tiger shoes for the baby panda. They are going to make the baby panda's heart feel super happy. *Kai xin!*

Let's put the tiger shoes in my heart box.

Oh, look at the street performer! He changes his masks to show how he feels. Tolee wants to make the baby panda a special mask with a happy face. It will make his heart feel super happy! *Kai xin!* Let's put the happy mask in my heart box.

I want to give the baby panda something special too. I know! I'll give him my heart box. It will make his heart feel super happy. *Kai xin!*

The baby panda loves all of his presents. "*Xie xie,*" he says. "Thank you."
Bu ke qi—you're welcome, baby panda! And guess what? The baby panda
finally got his name: *Xiao Xi Gua*—"little watermelon."

"*Wo jiao* Xiao Xi Gua!*" he says proudly. That means, "My name is Little
Watermelon."

I'm so glad we came to China. We met
Gu nai nai, we tried a lot of new things,
and we made a new friend. You really
helped Xiao Xi Gua today.
You make my heart feel super happy.
Zai jian! Good-bye!